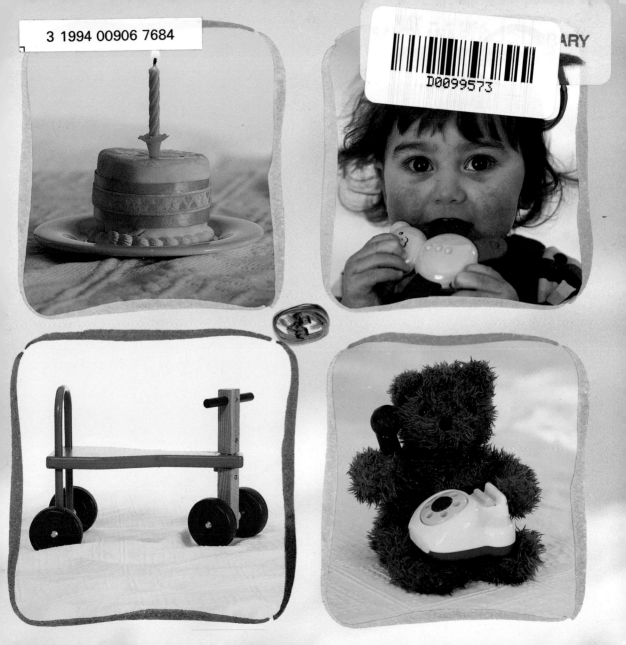

For Jackie B.

Aladdin Books
Macmillan Publishing Company
866 Third Avenue, New York, NY 10022
Maxwell Macmillan Canada

First Aladdin Books edition 1994

Copyright © 1993 by Fiona Pragoff

First published in Great Britain 1993
by Victor Gollancz
A Cassell imprint
Villiers House, 41/47 Strand, London WC2N 5JE

1 2 3 4 5 6 7 8 9 10

ISBN 0-689-71813-6

Printed in Hong Kong

Fiona Pragoff

IT'S FUN
TO BE ONE

ALADDIN BOOKS
Macmillan Publishing Company New York
Maxwell Macmillan Canada Toronto
Maxwell Macmillan International New York Oxford Singapore Sydney

When you are one
You have lots of fun.

You can brush your own hair
And clean your new teeth.

You want to talk

And make lots of noise.

You can drink from your cup
And feed yourself.

You look at your books

And go where you want to,

And after your bath
It's time for bed.